D1199070

The Tigers Next Door

Written and illustrated by Graham Percy

Derrydale Books
New York

There was once a happy family of
elephants who lived a carefree life on
the bottom shelf of the toy cupboard.

The two children, Annie and Arthur,
spent most of their time playing outdoors
in their big garden.

But – oh dear – one day,
the Elephants woke up
to find that a fence had
been put right through the
middle of their lovely lawn.

Their new neighbors, Mr. and Mrs.
Tiger, were most unfriendly and
had no time for Annie and Arthur.

Every morning, when the Elephants
came out to play, they found the Tigers
busy tidying their end of the shelf.

After their work, Mr. and Mrs. Tiger sat down for a quiet cup of tea.

In the afternoons, they took a nap and woke up just in time to make dinner.

Each morning, Annie and Arthur
called out to the Tigers, "Good morning.
Would you like to play with us today?"

"Certainly not," they always replied.
"We're far too busy."

Annie and Arthur continued to play their usual games. They tried to be careful, but, however hard they tried, they kept knocking down the fence and hitting their ball into the Tigers' garden.

It wasn't long before the Tigers started grumbling. "You useless little lumps keep making a mess of all our hard work," they complained.

Well, Arthur and Annie didn't like
being called "useless little lumps". They
sat by the pond and thought about how
they could show the Tigers that they
could be helpful. "I know," said Annie.
"Let's water their garden for them."

"That's a great idea," said Arthur.
"Let's do it right away."

In his hurry to stand up, he tripped
over Annie and they both tumbled into
the pond. Water splashed everywhere.

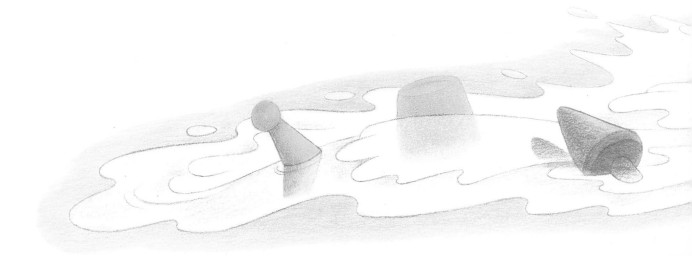

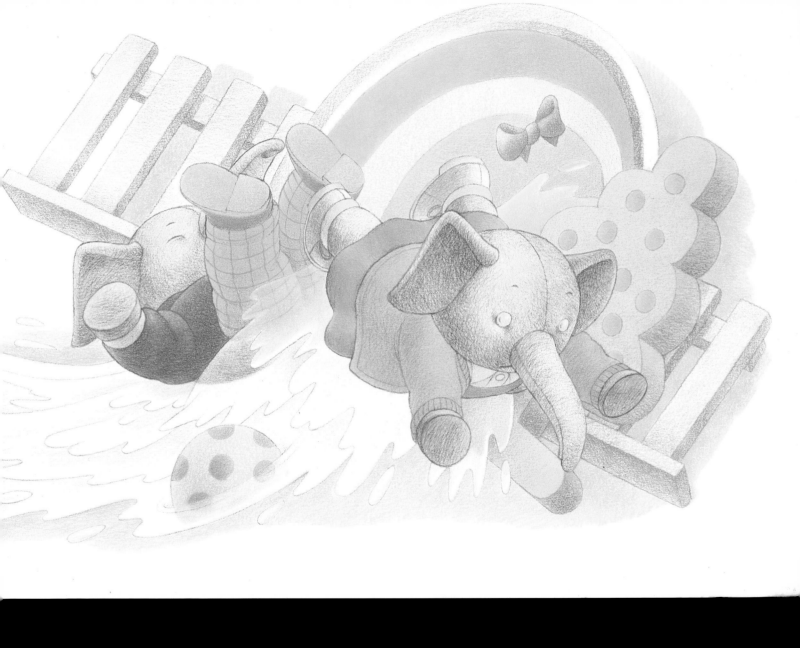

"Now see what you've done!"
snapped Mr. Tiger. "You've flooded our
garden and spoiled our shiny kitchen floor."

"Go away," he snarled. "Don't let me
see you outside again today."
Annie and Arthur ran home. They
sat on their beds and began to cry.

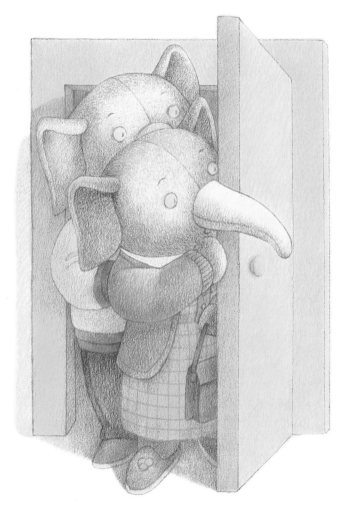

Mr. and Mrs. Elephant came in to see what all the commotion was about.

"Don't cry," said Mrs. Elephant, when she saw what had happened. "It won't take long to make everything alright again."

"I've just seen the Tigers go out shopping.
Go and see what you can do while they're out."

The elephants dried their tears and
quickly went next door.

Annie sucked up water with her trunk

and squirted it back into the pond, while
Arthur polished the kitchen floor.

He swirled around first on one foot
and then on the other, using one of his
mother's big, soft cloths.

They had just finished when Mr. and
Mrs. Tiger reappeared with full baskets.

"Oh my," purred Mrs. Tiger, "what
a surprise! I can see you're not so
useless after all."

She then whispered something to Mr.
Tiger, who grinned from ear to ear.

"We're going inside for a moment. While we're gone, move one piece of the fence to each end of the garden."

The little Elephants did as they were told, wondering what on earth the Tigers were up to.

It didn't take them long to find out.
Mr. and Mrs. Tiger came out, each
holding a hockey stick.

"Are you ready to play?" they asked.

Annie and Arthur didn't need to be
asked twice. For the rest of the day, they
all played a wonderful game of hockey.

The Tigers played so hard that the
poor little Elephants were completely
tired out! And, early the next morning,

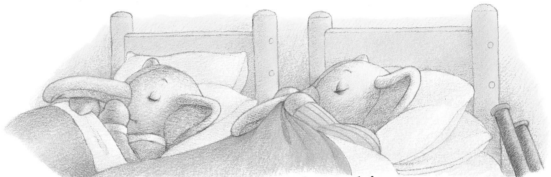

instead of cleaning, and working
in the garden, Mr. and Mrs. Tiger
were out practicing while Arthur and
Annie were still fast asleep in their beds!

This 1986 edition published by Derrydale Books, distributed by Crown Publishers, Inc.,
225 Park Avenue South, New York, New York 10003.

Conceived, designed and produced by Conran Octopus Limited, 28-32 Shelton Street, London WC2 9PH

ISBN 0-517-63110-5

Barcelona. Dep. Leg. B-21284-1986

hgfedcba